#22 Palms-Rancho Park Branch Library
2920 Overland Avenue
Los Angeles, CA 90064

#22 PALMS RANCHO PARK

You're MEAN, Lily Jean!

Frieda Wishinsky   illustrated by Kady MacDonald Denton

XZ
W

Albert Whitman & Company
Chicago, Illinois

The illustrations in this book were first sketched with a light (H) pencil,
then painted using Winsor & Newton watercolors.
They were finished with acrylic ink lines, oil crayon accents,
occasional gouache, and a dash of salt.

The text type was set in 28 point Aunt Mildred.

Library of Congress Cataloging-in-Publication Data

Wishinsky, Frieda.
You're mean, Lily Jean! / Frieda Wishinsky ; illustrated by Kady MacDonald Denton.
p. cm.
Summary: Sisters Carly and Sandy have always played together, but when Lily Jean moves in next door she
only wants to play with Sandy, and insists that if Carly joins them she must be a baby, or a cow, or a dog.
ISBN 978-0-8075-9476-6
[1. Sisters—Fiction. 2. Play—Fiction. 3. Behavior—Fiction.] I. Denton, Kady MacDonald, ill. II. Title.
III. Title: You are mean, Lily Jean!

PZ7.W78032You 2011
[E]—dc22
2010027028

Text copyright © 2009 by Frieda Wishinsky.
Illustrations copyright © 2009 by Kady MacDonald Denton.
First published in Canada by North Winds Press.
Published in 2011 by Albert Whitman & Company.
All rights reserved. No part of this book may be reproduced or transmitted in any form or by any means,
electronic or mechanical, including photocopying, recording, or by any information storage and retrieval
system, without permission in writing from the publisher. Printed in China.
10 9 8 7 6 5 4 3 2 1 BP 15 14 13 12 11

For more information about Albert Whitman & Company,
visit our web site at www.albertwhitman.com.

For my Suzie
— F.W.

For Eila
— K.M.D.

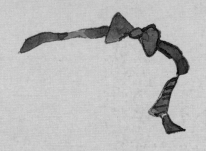

Carly always played with her big sister, Sandy.
They played dragons and knights.
They played explorers and pirates.
They played mountain climbers and astronauts.

Then Lily Jean moved in next door.

Lily Jean wore shiny red shoes and a puffy red skirt. She had a red ribbon in her long brown hair.

"I can play the xylophone and drums," she told them. "I can skate backwards and stand on my head."

"Wow!" said Sandy. "That's good."

"I know," said Lily Jean. "Let's play house."

"Can I play, too?" Carly asked.

"No," said Lily Jean.

"Let her play," said Sandy.

"Well... she can play, but only if she's the baby," said Lily Jean.

"Okay, I'll be the baby," Carly agreed.

"Good," said Lily Jean. "Now crawl, baby, and follow us wherever we go."

Carly sighed. She didn't want to crawl, but she wanted to play. So she crawled around after Sandy and Lily Jean.

The next day Lily Jean came over. "Come on, Sandy. Let's play cowgirls," she said.

"Can I play cowgirls, too?" asked Carly.

"You can be the cow," said Lily Jean.

"I don't want to be the cow. I want to be a cowgirl."

"Maybe we can have three cowgirls," said Sandy.

"Three cowgirls are too many," said Lily Jean. "Carly has to be the cow. The cow goes moo and eats grass."

Carly made a face. She did not want to moo
or eat grass, but Lily Jean said she had to if
she wanted to play. So she did.

The next day Lily Jean said, "Let's play king and queen. I'll be the king. Sandy will be the queen and Carly will be the dog."

"I don't want to be a dog," said Carly.

"Let's make Carly a lady-in-waiting," suggested Sandy.

"No. We need a dog," said Lily Jean.

"But I don't want to be a dog."

"Then you can't play," said Lily Jean.

Carly stomped away. Why does Sandy want to play
with Lily Jean anyway? she thought. Lily Jean is mean.
If only . . .

"Okay," said Carly, hurrying back. "I'll be the dog."
"Good," said Lily Jean. "Now follow us."
So Carly followed them to the picnic table.

"Dogs under the table," said Lily Jean.

"You don't have to go under the table," whispered Sandy.

"I want to," said Carly. And she crouched under the table.

Lily Jean tossed Carly a bone. "Now say bow-wow."
But instead of saying bow-wow, Carly grabbed
Lily Jean's shoe and ran.

"Hey, come back!" shouted Lily Jean.

"Bow-wow!" said Carly, as she ran to the side
of the house.

"Make your stupid sister give me back my shoe," snapped Lily Jean.

"My sister is not stupid," said Sandy.

"Yes, she is," shouted Lily Jean. "She took my shoe!"

"Your shoe is in the sandbox," said Carly.

"What?" screamed Lily Jean. "Why did you put it there?"

"I didn't. The dog did," said Carly.

"You can't be a dog ever again," said Lily Jean, hobbling toward the sandbox. "Come on, Sandy. Let's go to my house and play."

Sandy shook her head. "No."
"No? Why not?" said Lily Jean.

"I'm playing with Carly."

Carly beamed. "Do you want to play circus?"

Sandy smiled. "I'll be a tightrope walker," she said.

"And I'll be a lion tamer," said Carly.

"I want to play, too," said Lily Jean.

"No," said Carly.

"Please," said Lily Jean. "I can be a clown. I can be an elephant. I can be the lady who gets shot out of the cannon. I can be anything you want."

"Can you be nice?" asked Carly.
"I can be very nice," said Lily Jean.

Carly and Sandy looked at each other.
They looked at Lily Jean.

"Then follow us," said Carly.
And Lily Jean did.